Prommy Meets Her Match

An Unofficial Story for Shopkins Collectors

The Unofficial Shopkins Collectors #2

Prommy Meets Her Match

An Unofficial Story for Shopkins Collectors

Kenley Shay

Sky Pony Press
New York

First Edition

10 9 8 7 6 5 4 3 2 1

Library of Congress Control Number: 2015941430

Special thanks to Erin L. Falligant.

Cover illustration and design by Jan Gerardi

Print ISBN: 978-1-5107-0374-2
Ebook ISBN: 978-1-5107-0375-9

Printed in Canada

Chapter One

"Cool!" said Bella and Ava—at the exact same time.

"Horseback riding lessons," Bella whispered, gazing at the poster hanging in the window of Teasley Toys. In the picture, a teenaged girl rode a reddish-brown quarter horse, his coat gleaming in the sunlight.

"What?" said her twin sister, Ava, taking a step back. "No, not that one! This one." She pointed to the other sign in the window that read:

FALL FESTIVAL

Costume Contest!

Prizes awarded for best individual and group costumes

Bella glanced at the festival poster, but her eyes quickly flickered back to that horse. He had a white patch on his forehead. She could almost imagine reaching out and touching it. Would it be soft? Would he nicker at her like horses do in movies and TV shows?

"We can't take horseback riding lessons, Bella," said Ava, snapping her sister out of her daydream. "We're already in dance class, and Mom says we can only do one thing a season. Wouldn't you rather dance than ride horses?"

What Bella *wanted* to say was, "No! Riding horses would be so much more fun. Especially *this* horse." But Ava was right: they were already in dance. In fact, they'd just come from dance class, their pink leotards reflecting back at them in the shop window. So, instead, Bella said quietly, "Dance is okay, I guess."

Ava barely heard her sister; she was so focused on the fall festival poster. "It's next Saturday night! That doesn't give us a lot of time to put together costumes. What should we dress up as?"

Bella shrugged. *Horseback riders?* she wanted to say. *Cowgirls? Rodeo queens?* But she knew Ava wouldn't appreciate those suggestions.

The poster showed kids dressed up like princesses and superheros. Ava seemed really focused on those princess gowns. "It looks like they're at prom," she said in a dreamy voice, pointing at one bell-shaped dress.

Bella nodded. Their older cousin, Hannah, had just gone to her first prom, a high school dance where she wore a sparkly dress with a poufy skirt. The dress was pretty, but Bella kept wondering how Hannah could even fit in the car with a skirt that big!

Just then, the door to Teasley Toys opened with a *jingle*, and a red-haired girl with a freckled face popped out. "Ava! Bella! What are you doing here?"

It was Maggie, whose grandparents owned the toy shop. She was nine, a year younger than Ava and Bella, and the leader of one of their favorite clubs: the Shopkins Kids Club. They met every Friday at Teasley Toys to buy and trade Shopkins.

The door opened wider, and an older woman with short gray hair and lavender glasses leaned over Maggie's shoulder. "C'mon in, girls!" she called out. Then she frowned. "But wait, aren't you a day early?"

Ava laughed. "We're not here for the Shopkins Kids Club meeting, Gran. We're just walking home from dance lessons."

I wish she really was our gran, thought Bella. She thought it every time she saw Mrs. Teasley, who had such kind eyes. She really was as sweet and caring as Gran Jam, the Shopkin she'd gotten her nickname from. And she seemed to like it when all the girls called her "Gran."

"Dance class? That explains the matching outfits," Maggie said, pointing at the leotards Ava and Bella were wearing.

We don't really match, thought Bella. Sure, their leotards were both pink. But Bella's dance skirt was purple, not magenta like the one Ava wore.

"Speaking of outfits, are you going to the fall festival?" asked Ava, pointing at the poster. "Bella and I are trying to figure out what to wear."

"I want to go," said Maggie. "But Max and I have no idea what we're going to wear yet, either." Max was Maggie's little brother, and he looked a lot like her—with the same ginger-red hair and freckles. "Max will probably want to be a superhero, like always."

"I wish Bella and I could wear prom dresses to the party," said Ava, checking out the princess dresses in the poster again. "Mom could even sew them for us. But prom dresses aren't really costumes. Who would we be dressing up as?"

Maggie giggled. "You could go as Prommy," she suggested.

Prommy? At first Bella didn't get the joke. Then she remembered: Prommy was one of the Shopkins, a tiny high-heeled shoe. She and Ava had both versions of it in their Shopkins collection—the pink one and the yellow one.

Ava's eyes lit up as though Maggie had just handed her a winning lottery ticket. She started jumping up and down, and a dark curl sprang loose from the bun on the top of her head.

"That's it!" she said. "We'll dress up like Shopkins! We'll wear prom dresses. I'll be the pink Prommy and Bella can be the yellow Prommy. It's perfect!"

Not really, thought Bella. She wasn't crazy about the idea of wearing a prom dress. Those skirts were so big! She was sure she wouldn't be able to walk around without knocking into things—and other people. *You can't ride your bike in a skirt like that,* she thought. *And you sure can't ride a horse.*

But now Maggie had latched on to the idea, too. "Ooh, we should *all* dress up like Shopkins!

Maybe we could win the group prize. I wonder which Shopkin I should be. . . ." She gazed off into the distance for a moment and then said, "Oh, I know! I'll be right back."

Maggie disappeared into the toy store and popped back out twenty seconds later. She was carrying a lampshade.

"Maggie, what on earth?" Gran called from behind the counter.

"Just a sec, Gran," said Maggie. "I'll bring it right back—I promise." As soon as the door shut behind her, she turned to face Ava and Bella and promptly placed the lampshade on her head.

"Who am I?" she asked, her voice muffled by the shade.

"I have no idea," said Ava, giggling.

As Maggie tried to get the wobbly shade to sit straight on her head, all Bella could do was laugh. But when she finally got the words out, she said, "You're . . . Lana Lamp."

"Yes!" said Maggie. "How's that for a bright idea?" she asked, bending her fingers like quotation marks when she said the word *bright*.

Ava groaned at the joke, but Bella cracked up again. Then they heard a knock on the window. Gran was waving her hand at Maggie to come back inside.

"Who's there?" asked Maggie, trying to get the lampshade off her head. "Ouch!" Some of her hair was stuck.

"Gran wants her shade back," said Ava.

"She can have it! It's not very comfortable."

Maybe, that's because it's not made for your head, Bella thought, smiling. But at least Maggie had helped her forget about her own costume for a little bit—the Prommy dress that Ava had chosen for her.

"C'mon," said Ava. "We'd better get home before Mom starts to worry."

As Maggie waved good-bye and stepped back into the shop, Bella took one last look at that horse poster. *No horseback riding lessons for me,* she thought sadly. And no horseback riding costume, either—unless she could find a Shopkin in her collection that had *something* to do with horses.

Bella thought about the costume while she walked, wishing she'd get struck with a "bright idea" like Maggie's. But the only thing that struck were raindrops. She ran faster down the sidewalk toward home.

Chapter Two

Chirp, chirp, chirp . . .

Bella slapped her hand over the clock, still half asleep. Usually Ava got up first and turned off the alarm, but today she was still in bed—her dark curls matted against the side of her head.

"Ava?" asked Bella, crossing the rug between their twin beds to nudge her sister's shoulder.

Ava groaned. "My . . . throat . . . hurts," she said, swallowing hard.

Bella pulled her hand away. "Oh. I'll go get Mom."

Bella slid her feet into her slippers and padded down the long hall toward the kitchen.

Mom was already there, her dark hair pulled into a ponytail. She was standing over the pancake griddle.

"There's my girl," she said, grinning at Bella. "What's wrong, sleepyhead?"

"Ava's sick," Bella said, fighting a yawn. "Her throat hurts."

"Oh, dear." Mom turned down the griddle. "I'll go check on her. But why don't you go ahead and eat, sweetie." She pulled out a chair at the table where she'd already placed a short stack of steaming pancakes.

Bella had nearly eaten two by the time Mom came back.

"She's definitely sick," said Mom, shaking a thermometer in her hand. "Which means you'll probably get it, too. You two share just about everything."

A bite of pancake stuck in Bella's throat. *Great,* she thought, forcing it down. *Now I have that to look forward to.*

She pushed the pancakes away and got up to wash her sticky fingers. As she stood at the sink, Bella let the hot water run longer than usual, soaping her hands again and again.

You'll probably get it, too, her mom had said.

Not if I can help it, thought Bella, reaching for the towel. This was one thing she definitely *didn't* want to share.

After school, Bella rode her bike to Teasley Toys—alone. It felt strange, not following Ava down the bike lane. Ava was the one who usually looked both ways at street crossings. Ava waved at people on the sidewalk and said hello, so Bella—following behind—didn't have to.

Today, Bella rode extra carefully, making sure to stop at all the stop signs. And when she passed the dance studio just as one of the teachers was propping open the door, Bella raised her hand—just a little—and waved.

As she locked up her blue bike in the rack in front of Teasley Toys, Bella couldn't help noticing how empty the rack seemed. Ava's pink bike was usually there first, parked right beside Bella's. But not today.

"Where's your sister?" someone called in a deep voice. It was Papa, Maggie's grandpa, stepping out of the shop with an armful of flattened brown boxes. He looked at Bella as if he wasn't quite sure which sister she was—or which sister was missing.

"She's . . . ," Bella began in a whisper. "She's sick," she said in a louder voice, checking to see if her throat was sore. Not yet, thank goodness!

"That's too bad," said Papa. "Well, let's hope you don't get it, too. I know you girls share everything," he added with a wink. Then he walked the boxes to the car at the curb and searched his pocket for his keys.

Bella couldn't even smile. *Not funny,* she thought. *I wish people would stop saying that!*

Now, all she could think about was getting sick. As soon as Papa's back was turned, she felt her neck to make sure it wasn't swollen. She placed her hand against her forehead, the way her mom always did, to check for fever. And when she pulled open the door of Teasley Toys, she used her shirt hem to grab the door handle. If she wasn't sick yet, she didn't want to get any new germs off that handle. *Better safe than sorry*, she thought.

Max was the first person to greet her inside. "Bella!" he said, swooping his toy airplane in her direction. Somehow, Max could always tell Ava and Bella apart, even if Papa couldn't.

"Hi, Max," Bella said, dodging the plane.

When he offered her a turn with it, she dodged that, too. "Um, no thanks," she said quickly, noticing how Max kept wiping his runny nose with the back of his hand. That airplane was probably full of germs. *Little kids want to share everything, too,* she realized. But today Bella was determined to stay healthy.

"Hey, where's Ava?" asked Maggie, stepping into the shop from the back room.

"She's sick," Bella said again, feeling like a robot repeating the same words over and over.

Maggie furrowed her brow. "Really? Well, you'll probably— "

"Don't say it!" Bella interrupted, more loudly than she meant to.

Maggie took a step back. "Sheesh. I was just going to say that you'll probably want to take your Shopkins home instead of opening them here. I mean, because you and Ava share everything."

There it is, thought Bella with a sigh.

It was true, though. She and Ava shared their entire Shopkins collection. Every time they bought a new pack, they opened it together. And if they were going to trade Shopkins with other members in the club, they had to decide on that together, too.

As Bella flipped through the packages of Shopkins in the bin by the counter, she didn't feel as excited as she normally did on Friday afternoons. If she couldn't open the package here, what fun would the club meeting be?

She quickly paid Gran with her money and the money she had pulled out of Ava's pink piggybank this morning. She held Ava's dollar bills carefully because they were probably loaded with sore-throat germs. As she dropped them on the counter, one by one, Gran gave her a funny look. But Bella ignored it. She didn't want to have to tell Gran that Ava was sick. She knew exactly what Gran would say.

After paying, Bella hurried into the back room with her Shopkins, hoping she wasn't the last one there.

Gabby and Ellie were already sitting on the rug. And Maggie was there, too, helping Max sort through his plastic bag of Shopkins.

"Ooh, I've got it," said Maggie, pulling out a tiny loaf of bread. "You can be Slick Breadstick!"

Max took the Shopkin from her fingers and studied the little guy. "Could I wear a hat like that?" he asked.

"Sure," said Maggie. "Gran can sew a beret to your costume. I think you'd look pretty cool with a mustache, too."

Max smiled slowly. "Yeah, that's what I'll be."

Gabby and Ellie were talking about costume ideas, too. Maggie must have told them about the fall festival.

"I'll be Bun Bun Slipper!" said Ellie. She held up two fingers on either side of her head and grinned, showing a gap in her smile where she must have lost a tooth.

Her older sister, Gabby, laughed. "I think that's a great idea. And you already have bunny ears from Easter, remember?"

"Oh, yeah!" said Ellie, bouncing on her knees. "What are you going to be, Gabby?"

Gabby shook her head. "I don't know. I can't think of anything yet."

Maggie pointed toward the lamp in the corner of the storage room. "I could always find you another lampshade," she said, giggling.

"No thanks," said Gabby. "I think one Lana Lamp is enough!" Then she turned toward Bella. "How's your Prommy costume coming?" she asked.

Bella shrugged, feeling her cheeks burn as they often did when someone asked her a question. "Okay," she finally said.

Maggie checked the clock and said, "Oh! We're late! We should get started." She flipped open the green notebook in front of her and said, "Bella, you get to open your Shopkins first this week. Oh, wait . . . are you taking yours home to open with Ava?"

Bella looked down at the five-pack in her hands. There was only one yellow blind bag in this package, tucked way down at the bottom. And even though she should wait for Ava, she really, *really* wanted to open it.

She licked her lips and said, "I think . . . I'll open it here."

"Yay!" said Ellie, clapping. "It's more fun that way."

So Bella carefully tore the plastic shell off the package and reached into the bottom for the yellow pouch. Gabby handed her a pair of scissors, and she snipped away the corner of the pouch. Then she pushed out the mystery Shopkin.

A little white cowboy boot dropped to the floor.

"What's that?" asked Max, who looked like he was dying to snatch it up.

"Ooh," said Maggie. "Betty Boot! Ava will love that one."

Not as much as I do, Bella thought instantly. Sure, Ava loved the shoe Shopkins. But this one was different. This one was a cowboy boot, the kind a cowgirl would wear—the kind a girl might wear if she was riding *horses.*

And that was when Bella had her bright idea.

"What is it?" asked Gabby, noticing that Bella was about to burst.

"I know what my costume is going to be," said Bella, the words flowing from her mouth faster than ever.

"A Prommy dress?" asked Maggie, puzzled.

"No," said Bella with certainty. "I'm going to be a Betty Boot cowgirl."

"Fun!" said Ellie.

"Super fun," said Gabby, smiling.

"Great idea!" said Maggie.

"Do you know how to ride a horse?" asked Max as he hopped up from the floor and started galloping around the room.

Bella shook her head. "But I want to learn. I want to take lessons."

Maggie sat up straight. "I know a girl who's teaching them this fall," she said. "Did you see her poster in the window of the shop?"

Bella sucked in her breath. "You *know* that girl?" she asked, picturing the teenager riding on top of the beautiful rust-colored horse.

"Sure," said Maggie. "She's Gran's neighbor. That's why she asked Gran if she could hang the poster here. I sometimes visit her and her horse, Apple, on Saturday mornings."

Bella's heart sped up. "Apple? Is that the horse in the poster?"

Maggie smiled. "Yup. He's named Apple because he's so red."

"No," said Max, still galloping in circles around the room. "It's because he likes to eat apples, Maggie."

Maggie rolled her eyes. "That's *part* of it, Max. But all horses like apples. Now sit down, would you?"

Bella was barely listening. She didn't know what was more exciting: her Betty Boot costume idea or the fact that her friend Maggie *knew* the horse in that poster and got to visit him sometimes.

Then Maggie said the most exciting thing of all: "Maybe you could come visit Apple with me tomorrow, Bella. Do you want to?"

Bella was speechless, not because she was feeling shy, but because she couldn't think of anything in the whole world that she would rather do than go visit the horse. She nodded so hard, she almost made herself dizzy.

Tomorrow, she thought happily. *Tomorrow!*

Chapter Three

"Ouch!" Bella was trying to pull her thick, curly hair into a ponytail when the hair band broke, snapping against her finger.

Ava lifted her head from her pillow, groaned, and set it back down. "Where . . . are . . . you going?" she asked, wincing with each word. She was definitely still sick.

Bella had been trying to sneak out. She didn't want to tell Ava she was going to meet Apple. Ava didn't love horses as much as Bella did. Would she just remind Bella, again, that she couldn't take lessons this fall?

Bella thought fast. "I'm . . . riding bikes with Maggie," she said. It was true: she and Maggie were going to ride their bikes to the horse stable. But Bella had never ridden bikes with a friend without Ava going, too.

Ava must have been thinking the same thing. She opened her mouth as if she were about to ask a question, and then closed it again. Maybe it just didn't seem worth the pain and effort. She rolled over and sighed.

Bella quickly tiptoed out of the room, closing the door behind her. As she let go of the doorknob, she wiped her hand on her pants. She was still trying to steer clear of germs. Whatever bug Ava had was a bad one. Bella would have to work hard not to get it!

The crisp fall air filled Bella's lungs as she biked behind Maggie on the leaf-covered path. If she narrowed her eyes, Bella could almost imagine that she was riding Apple instead. She pictured galloping through the woods on that beautiful horse, feeling the wind in her hair. As she reached out to stroke his red mane, he whinnied back at her, as if saying . . .

Oops! A bump in the road made her bike wobble, jolting her out of her daydream. She tightened her grip on her handlebars.

Soon, the girls turned onto the long gravel driveway that led to the stable. A white fence enclosed a lush green pasture with small fruit trees lining one side. As Bella hopped off her bike to walk it the rest of the way, she saw apples on the ground.

So, Max was right! Apple does eat apples, she thought happily, picking one up and putting it in her pocket.

Just then, she heard a soft *whinny*, and a horse stepped out from behind an apple tree. He was on the other side of the fence, but he was staring right at Bella. She felt her heart skip a beat.

"Apple?" she said softly, noticing the white patch on his forehead.

The horse took a step backward, as if he was afraid of her.

"No, that's not Apple," said Maggie, wheeling her bike up beside Bella. "That's Starburst."

"But it looks just like the horse in the poster!" said Bella. She remembered every detail, from the sheen of the horse's red coat to the white fur above his eyes.

"They're brothers," said Maggie. "But I can tell them apart."

"How?" asked Bella, amazed.

Maggie laughed. "The same way I can tell you and Ava apart," she said, laughing. "You two act totally different!"

Bella smiled. *I guess that's true,* she thought. *But don't all horses act alike?*

She didn't say that out loud. She didn't want to offend Starburst.

"I'll show you," said Maggie. She leaned her bike against the fence and reached down to pick up a red apple. As she held it out to Starburst, he lifted his nose to sniff the air. But as soon as Maggie took a step toward him, he took another step backward.

Then, from across the pasture, came a second horse trotting toward the fence. He nudged Starburst out of the way and then gently—but quickly—gobbled the apple right out of Maggie's hand. She laughed and stroked his nose.

"See?" she said. "Guess who this is?"

"Apple," said Bella, grinning.

"Yup. He's braver than Starburst and likes apples way more," said Maggie. "You can feed him one if you want."

Bella's heart raced. She'd never been this close to a horse before, but she wasn't going to miss the opportunity. She stepped toward the fence and slowly extended the apple on her flattened palm, just as Maggie had done. The horse took the apple with his soft lips. He ate it in a few chomps and came back and sniffed her hand, nuzzling her palm with his mouth.

Bella laughed. "It tickles!" she said. She reached up with her other hand and gently stroked Apple's brown nose.

"Do you want to know how else I can tell these two apart?" asked Maggie, leaning against the fence. "The white patch on Starburst's forehead is shaped like a star."

Now that the horses were side-by-side, Bella could see that the white fur on their foreheads *did* look different. Starburst had a white star, and Apple had more of a triangle. Bella wondered if other people could see tiny differences like that between her and Ava, too.

"Hey, looks like Apple found some friends!" a cheery voice called. A blonde teenager walked toward them with long strides, her jeans tucked into riding boots.

"Hi, Jessie!" called Maggie. "This is Bella, the horse-crazy girl I was telling you about."

Horse-crazy? Bella was about to argue, but then realized Maggie was kind of right. How could she not be crazy about a horse like Apple?

Jessie laughed. "Nice to meet you, Bella," she said. "I was horse-crazy when I was your age. I still am." She flipped her long braid behind her shoulder and extended her hand to shake Bella's.

Bella smiled shyly and shook Jessie's hand, noticing that Jessie was wearing horseshoe earrings. Bella liked her instantly, almost as much as she liked Apple.

"Jessie rides in competitions," said Maggie proudly, as if she were talking up her best friend.

"Really?" asked Bella.

"Sometimes," said Jessie. "Apple and I used to do a lot more of them. Want to see some pictures? You can check them out while I clean Apple's stall." She nodded her head sideways toward the stable.

"Sure!" said Maggie, reaching for her bike.

Bella shrugged in agreement, although she was more excited about seeing Apple's stall than about seeing the photos.

As the girls wheeled their bikes toward the stable, Apple trotted along the fence beside them. He nickered as if to say, "Hey, wait for me!"

Inside the stable, there were three stalls for horses. Across from the stalls, framed photos hung above hooks filled with tack.

"Look!" said Maggie, pointing toward the first photo.

Bella recognized Apple and Jessie right away. Jessie looked much younger, but she stood tall and proud beside Apple in her cowboy hat, white riding skirt, and white boots with gold tassels.

She's a real cowgirl! thought Bella, suddenly wishing she had a camera so she could take a picture of the picture. "Look at that outfit," she whispered.

Maggie's face broadened into a smile. "It's your Betty Boot costume!" she said.

Bella nodded. "I'm going to draw a picture of that for my mom. She can sew costumes pretty fast, but I don't know where I'm going to find a hat like that."

Maggie laughed. "I know where," she said. "My little brother's toy chest. He'd probably let you borrow it."

A loud *creak* made both girls whirl around. Jessie was pushing a wheelbarrow into the stable, a pitchfork and broom balanced across the top.

"That's the fun part of owning horses," she said, pointing toward the photos on the wall. "This is the not so fun part." She took the pitchfork out of the wheelbarrow and stepped into Apple's stall, sifting through the sawdust with the pitchfork.

"So, Bella," said Jessie while she worked, "Maggie says you might be interested in some horseback riding lessons. Is that true?"

Bella swallowed hard. "I want to take lessons," she said, "but my sister wants to take dance instead, so . . ." She picked at the edge of a fingernail.

"Your sister isn't into horses?" asked Jessie as she dropped a clump of manure into the wheelbarrow.

Bella giggled, thinking about how Ava would wrinkle up her nose if she were anywhere near horse manure. "She's not really into . . . that." Bella pointed toward the wheelbarrow.

Jessie laughed. "Not everyone is," she said. "And you're not into dance as much as your sister is?"

Bella shrugged. "Just not as much as horses."

Jessie nodded. "Horses are your passion," she said. "I get that."

Apple whinnied from the pasture beyond, as if to say, "Me, too."

Jessie leaned on her pitchfork and grinned. "Yes, we know you're there, Apple," she called to the horse. "We haven't forgotten about you. And we all know what *your* passion is."

At the same time, all three girls said, "Apples!"

Before leaving the stable, Bella took one more long look at Jessie's cowgirl costume in the photo on the wall. She wanted to memorize it so that she could draw it for her mom. She could hardly wait to get home to tell her about it!

Ava's not going to be happy about it, she thought. But she couldn't bear the idea of wearing a yellow Prommy dress to the party, not when she could have a Betty Boot costume like Jessie's.

As soon as she got home, she parked her blue bike carefully in the garage and pushed open the door to the kitchen. Dad was at the counter, eating a bologna sandwich. "Hey, Bella," he said, wiping mustard off his mouth with a paper towel.

"Where's Mom?" Bella asked quickly. When she saw the look on her dad's face, she said, "I mean, hi, Dad. How are you? And where's Mom?"

Her dad shook his head and laughed. "Downstairs," he said. "In the sewing room. I think she's got a surprise for you."

Bella felt a flutter of excitement at the word "surprise." Then she felt something else—dread. What kind of surprise would Mom have in the sewing room? Not a Betty Boot costume. She didn't even know about that idea yet. So what could it be, except . . . the Prommy dresses. Uh-oh.

Bella walked slowly down the stairs, her legs feeling as heavy as tree trunks. Her mom must have heard her coming because she met Bella at the bottom of the stairs waving something yellow and shiny on a hanger. It was a tea-length, satin ball gown in a sunny shade of yellow.

"Wait, there's more!" said Mom. She turned the dress around to show the big bow at the back. "What do you think? Do you love it?"

It was beautiful. It was perfectly Prommy. And yet, Bella didn't love it. A teensy part of her—the little girl part—wanted to tear that dress to pieces.

That's Ava's costume, she wanted to say. *It's not mine!* Except it *wasn't* Ava's costume. Ava would never wear yellow if she could wear pink. Bella sighed and used every ounce of energy she could muster to turn her frowning face into a smile. "Thanks, Mom," she said in her robot voice. "It's really pretty."

Luckily, Mom was too excited by her own creation to notice Bella's mood. She was already jogging to the sewing room to get the second dress, the pink one. "Let's show Ava. Maybe it'll make her feel better, poor thing."

Bella hid behind the yellow dress as she walked up the stairs, hoping her dad wouldn't still be there eating his sandwich. She didn't think she could fake excitement a second time today. She rounded the corner slowly, peeked around the dress, and saw that the coast was clear.

Ava was still sleeping when Mom knocked on the bedroom door and gently pushed it open. "Ava, honey," she said. "I have a surprise for you."

Ava opened her eyes slowly and glanced at the pink dress. She perked up for about half a second, looking like her old self. But as soon as she tried to swallow, a flash of pain spread across her face.

"Oh, honey," said Mom, hanging the dress on the doorknob. "Is your throat still sore?"

Ava nodded.

"Can you talk at all?" asked Mom.

Ava just shook her head.

Ava can't talk? Well, that's a first, thought Bella.

She felt bad for her sister, but she felt bad for herself, too. *I know just how it feels to have something really important to say—and to not be able to speak a word of it.*

Chapter Four

Ding-dong!

Bella quickly took her finger away from the doorbell. It was so loud! She heard the door unlatch from the inside, and then . . . a giant lampshade appeared in the doorway.

"Maggie?" Bella asked, giggling.

"Bella?" came Maggie's muffled voice. "I thought you were going to be Gabby."

"I thought you were . . . Lana Lamp," joked Bella.

"Oh, good!" said Maggie. "Do you think this shade works for my costume?" She spun from side to side so that Bella could get a better look.

"I think it worked better on the lamp!" came her mother's voice from the living room. "Bring it back in here. *Now,* Margaret Josephine."

"Okay, okay," said Maggie, turning around to head back into the house. "I can't see very well through it anyway. C'mon, Bella." As Maggie wobbled her way back toward the living room, the shade clipped the corner of the doorway, bouncing her backward. "Ouch."

"Too big?" asked Bella as Maggie slid the shade carefully off her head.

"Maybe a little," Maggie admitted, handing the shade to her mom.

"How are you, Bella?" asked Maggie's mom. "Maggie's been 'shade shopping' all morning around the house. I'm following her, trying to make sure we still have lamps that work."

Maggie sighed. "Who knew that finding a shade to fit my head would be so hard?"

Her mom leaned over to kiss Maggie's ginger-colored hair. "It's a beautiful head. But maybe give it a rest for a while, okay? It's only Sunday—you have all week to finish your costume."

Maggie nodded. "How's your costume coming, Bella?"

Now it was Bella's turn to grumble. "It's done," she said. "Except, it's not a Betty Boot costume."

Maggie cocked her head. "What do you mean?"

Bella sighed and sank down on the edge of the couch. "Mom already finished the Prommy dresses. Now I *have* to wear one of them."

Maggie sat down beside her and dropped her chin into her hands. "I'm sorry. I guess nothing's really working out. You have a costume you don't want, I can't seem to make the costume I *do* want, and . . ."

Ding-dong!

"And Gabby can't even *think* of a costume!" said Maggie, jumping back up. "I bet that's her now. I told her I would help her come up with some ideas."

Bella followed Maggie to the entryway just as the doorbell rang again. Bella covered her ears. Why did it have to be so loud?

When Maggie opened the door, Gabby was standing with her hand raised as if mid-knock. "Oh, hi," she said, stepping inside. "Hi, Bella! I'm glad you're here, too. I need all the help I can get thinking of a costume." She raised a small purple case into the air. "I brought my tablet for ideas."

"I know another place where we'll find ideas," said Maggie. "Max's toy chest. He has all kinds of dress-up stuff in there. Some of it used to be mine."

"Cool," said Gabby. "Will your old dress-up stuff still fit, though?"

Maggie shrugged. "It'll fit at least as well as the two dozen lamp shades I tried on my head this morning."

The girls laughed as they followed her upstairs to Max's room.

It was obvious which bedroom was Max's. His walls were painted baby blue with a black train track border. In one corner, just beside the bunk beds, sat a red toy chest shaped like a train engine.

"Is Max here somewhere?" asked Bella, expecting the boy to pop out at them unexpectedly the way he usually did.

"No, he's down at the toy shop," said Maggie. "Gran and Papa got in a new shipment of train stuff today, and Max is helping them test it out." Then Maggie spotted the lamp in the corner. "Oh, look!" she said. "I haven't tried on this one yet."

She unscrewed the yellow shade from the top of the lamp and rested it on her head—or tried to. The shade was much too small.

"Well?" asked Maggie, turning first to Gabby and then to Bella for their reactions.

"You look . . ." Bella began, trying to be nice.

". . . like the cap on a toothpaste tube," Gabby finished. And she was right!

Bella clamped her hand over her mouth and laughed, hoping she wasn't hurting Maggie's feelings.

Maggie pretended to be annoyed, but she finally laughed, too, until the shade fell off her head. As she screwed it back onto the lamp, she nodded toward the toy box. "Go ahead," she said. "Dig in."

The toy chest held all kinds of treasures—a superhero cape, a monster mask, and a light-up sword. There was also a peach-colored tutu and a pink cat mask. When Gabby lifted a fireman helmet out of the box, something dropped into her lap.

"Eww," she said, flicking it onto the rug. It was a half-eaten toaster pastry.

"See!" said Maggie. "I told you that you'd get Shopkins costume ideas from Max's room. You could be Toasty Pop!"

Gabby wrinkled her nose and shook her head.

"Or Chris P Crackers?" asked Bella, brushing cracker crumbs off the superhero cape.

"No thanks!" said Gabby, laughing.

That's when Bella saw it—a flash of woven yellow. She carefully pulled a cowboy hat out from beneath the other toys. As she set it on her head, she knew immediately—it wasn't too big, and it wasn't too small. It fit her head perfectly.

"Oh, Bella," said Maggie, sinking down onto her knees. "It would have been great for your Betty Boot costume."

Gabby tucked a strand of dark hair behind one ear. "What do you mean, 'would have been'?" she asked, looking from Maggie to Bella and back again.

Bella didn't have the heart to explain it. So Maggie told Gabby about the Prommy costumes—how Bella would have to dress up like her sister even though she would much rather dress up as Betty Boot.

Gabby shook her head. "I'm sorry, Bella. That stinks." Then she smiled. "Let me get this straight. You have two costume ideas. And I still don't even have one!"

Gabby was trying to lighten the mood, but Bella just felt worse. She knew that having two costumes was better than none, but she would gladly change places with Gabby. At least Gabby got to decide what she wanted to wear instead of having someone else decide it for her. Bella took the hat off her head and tossed it back into the toy box.

Maggie's eyes wandered to the ceiling like they often did when she was thinking hard. "Wait, I've got it," she said suddenly. "Another bright idea!"

Bella sighed. "Is that another lampshade joke?" she asked. She didn't feel like laughing right now.

"What do you mean?" asked Gabby.

"You know," Bella explained quietly. "Maggie is a lamp. Lamps are bright. Maggie has bright ideas."

"Oh," said Gabby, giggling. "I get it."

"No," said Maggie, "I'm not trying to be funny. This idea is really brilliant!"

"Brilliant, like a light bulb?" asked Gabby, grinning.

Maggie shook her head. "Stop it!" The corner of her mouth twitched as if she were fighting a smile. "I'm being serious now. Here's what

I'm thinking: Bella has one costume too many, and Gabby still needs a costume. So, do the math. Do you get the same answer I do?"

Wait, thought Bella. *Does she want me to give my Prommy dress to Gabby to wear?*

"You mean I should wear Bella's Prommy dress?" Gabby asked at the same time. She half-smiled. She liked the idea; Bella could tell.

"Yes!" said Maggie. "It's perfect. What do you think, Bella? Or should I call you 'Betty Boot'?"

Bella slowly pulled the yellow cowboy hat back out of the box. *Could it work?* she wondered. *Will Mom and Ava be okay with it?*

She set the hat back on her head. "It's worth a try," she told Maggie with a smile.

Chapter Five

It was official—Ava had strep throat. When Mom and Ava came home from the doctor on Monday night, Mom was carrying a white bag from the pharmacy.

"Let's have you take your antibiotic right away," she said, pulling the pill bottle out of the bag and pouring a glass of water.

She handed a pill to Ava, who put it in her mouth and took a big gulp of water. When she swallowed, she grimaced, and some of the water dribbled out of the corners of her mouth.

"I know, honey," said Mom soothingly. "How about some ice cream to chase it down?"

Ava nodded. She looked miserable. And Bella was actually starting to miss the sound of her voice.

How can I tell her about the costumes now? Bella wondered. Mom said the antibiotics would start to work by tomorrow night. Hopefully, Ava would feel a little better by then. *I'll tell her tomorrow,* Bella decided.

"Do you want an ice cream cone, too?" Mom asked her, holding the ice cream scoop in her hand.

"Sure," said Bella. She opened the pantry to pull out the box of cones.

"Remember to wash your hands first," Mom reminded her. "Strep throat is really contagious. It's a miracle you haven't come down with it yet yourself."

It's not a miracle, thought Bella. *I've been working hard to make sure I don't!*

And she had just washed her hands a minute ago. But she washed them again—just in case.

On Tuesday night, Bella came home to a surprise.

"Hey, Bella!" said Ava. She was sitting at the kitchen counter, her curly hair still wet from a shower.

Bella dropped her dance bag on the floor and hurried across the kitchen. It was so good to hear Ava's voice again! But just before she gave her sister a big hug, Mom put her hands together in a time-out sign.

"Don't get too close," Mom warned. "The doctor said Ava may still be contagious for another day or two."

Ava rolled her eyes and patted the stool. "You can still sit next to me," she said. "I feel like I haven't talked to you in ages. How was dance class? And are you excited about the costume party? Ooh, we should try on our dresses!" Then she winced and put her hand to her throat.

"Careful, honey," said Mom. "Don't wear yourself out. Your body is still working on getting better, remember?"

Ava nodded. But she patted the stool again and pleaded with Bella using her eyes.

Bella hesitated. Ava wanted to talk about the costume party, and Bella just wasn't ready to do that yet. The thought of telling her sister that she'd chosen a different costume made her stomach flip-flop. Besides, she hadn't even really put together her cowgirl costume yet.

It'd be better to tell her after I have that all done, Bella thought. But what she said out loud was, "I have homework." Putting together a costume was *kind* of like homework.

"Ava's going to have a lot of homework to catch up on, too," said Mom. "Did you bring more home for her today?"

Bella nodded and fished through her backpack for Ava's red folder. As she set it on the counter, her sister sighed. "I think I'm starting to feel sick again. . . ." But she reached for a pencil from the cup by the sink.

Bella took that chance to hurry down the hall and into the bedroom. With Ava busy doing homework, Bella would have time to look through the closet they shared. Would she be able to find a white dress to wear with the cowboy hat? And did Ava have any western boots she could borrow?

An hour later, Bella had found some things that would have to do: an old white sundress and Ava's white ankle boots. *If I glue sequins to the dress and tie some gold tassels to the boots,* Bella thought, *this could work.* But doing those things would *take* work. And she'd need Ava's permission to wear the boots. She'd have to tell her about the costume sooner or later.

Bella glanced at the alarm clock by her bed. It was almost time for dinner. And, after that, she and Ava would be watching their favorite dance show. And then it would be bedtime, and

Ava really needed her sleep so that she could get healthy again.

So . . . Bella reasoned, *I should wait and tell her about the costumes tomorrow. What's one more day?*

Wednesday after school, Bella opened the front door and found a pink fairy in the living room. It took her a moment to recognize Ava in the middle of all that pink poufiness. She was wearing her Prommy dress, with pink high-heeled shoes and a pink headband. And her hair . . . something was different about it.

"What did you do to your hair?" Bella asked.

"I straightened it, silly!" said Ava. "With a straightening iron. Mom helped. Do you like it?"

Mom came out of the kitchen wiping her hands on a dishtowel.

"Someone is definitely feeling better today," she said. "Which means back to school tomorrow, little miss."

Ava groaned. "Who has time for school?" she said, her voice sounding clear and bright. "We have a party to plan for! Quick, Bella, get your Prommy costume on. I want to make sure we match."

Bella glanced back at the front door, wishing she could run right back out of the room. It was time to tell Ava the truth. But the words just wouldn't come.

"I'll help you change," said Ava, racing ahead to their bedroom. "C'mon!"

Bella followed her sister like she always did. It was as if Ava was a magnet and Bella was made out of metal. She wasn't running, but her legs were moving forward just the same.

The yellow Prommy dress hung from the bedroom doorknob. Ava carefully placed it on the bed and pulled the hanger out. "You know, Bella," she said, running her hand along the smooth yellow fabric, "I felt really weird this week."

"Because of strep throat, you mean?" asked Bella, untying her shoes.

"No," said Ava. "Because, for the first time in my whole life, I felt . . . alone." She sat on the bed beside the dress, her hands resting in her lap.

Bella slowly pulled off a shoe. "What do you mean?" she asked. Ava looked sad somehow, like she was carrying a heavy secret.

Ava sighed. "Well, you weren't here. You were going to dance lessons and to the Shopkins Kids Club meetings and even . . . riding bikes with Maggie." Ava looked away when she said that like the words kind of hurt. "And even when you were home, I never saw you. It was like you didn't want to be around me."

Because of germs! Bella wanted to shout. But she didn't. Ava was still talking.

"I felt," Ava began again, "like you were making new best friends. And I was . . ." She picked at a loose thread on the bedspread.

"You were what?" Bella nudged gently. She wasn't used to seeing Ava at a loss for words.

"I was *losing* my best friend," said Ava sadly.

She took a deep breath and shook her head, as though she was trying to shake off the sadness. "But now," she said, patting the yellow dress beside her, "we have the costume party to look forward to. And in our matching dresses, we'll be twins and best friends again—just like always."

Ava's smile made Bella's heart hurt. It was so good to see Ava feeling better. But now that Bella knew how lonely Ava had been feeling, how could she *not* wear the Prommy dress? She would just make her sister feel sad all over again!

So instead of telling Ava about the Betty Boot costume and about Gabby wearing the yellow Prommy dress, Bella did something else. She sat by her sister, put her arm around her shoulders, and said, “You’ll never lose your best friend, Ava.”

Ava smiled and put her head on Bella’s shoulder. “Thanks. But enough with the mushy stuff. Let’s try on your dress!”

Bella nodded and stood up. As she slipped off her jeans and stepped into the satiny dress, she remembered something: *If I wear this dress, Gabby won’t have a costume!* And with only three days till the party, it would be tough for Gabby to come up with one.

She’d have to get Gabby a message, but how?

Ava was already calling to Mom to plug in the flatiron. It was going to be a long night.

Chapter Six

"Don't rip your skirt!" said Mom, opening the door of the minivan. Ava stepped out onto the curb first, looking like a princess in her pink Prommy gown. Bella followed behind, trying not to wobble too much in her high-heeled shoes.

If only Mom had made the dresses longer . . . she thought. *Then I could have worn my sneakers, and no one would know!*

The front door of Teasley Toys opened, and Ellie hopped out. She wore bunny ears on her head and bunny slippers on her feet. "Who am I?" she squeaked.

"Bun Bun Slipper!" said Ava. "Pretty cute, Ellie."

Ellie flashed her gap-toothed smile and reached for Ava's hand, leading her back into Teasley Toys.

Instead of a Shopkins Kids Club this Friday night, the club was doing what Maggie called a "dress rehearsal." If they were going to win the group prize at the costume party, she'd said, they should try on their costumes a day early—just to be safe.

As Bella stepped into the shop, she spotted Maggie right away. She had on a berry-colored dress that flared out at the bottom like the base of Lana Lamp. And she was wearing the lampshade from Gran's storage room, the first one she'd ever tried on. But the shade had a giant dent in it.

"Max!" Maggie bellowed from beneath the shade. "Watch where you're going! This is the only lampshade that fits me." She took off the shade and tried to press the dented part back out.

But where was Max? Bella saw a long beige pillow rolling around on the floor, trying to get up. Max's face peered out of a hole near the bottom.

"See?" Ellie said to Ava. "I told you. Max is Slick Breadstick!"

Ava laughed. It was hard not to. Bella smothered a smile, too, when she saw the crooked paper mustache taped to Max's lip.

Max tried to stand up, but the pillow was so big that he could barely crawl to his knees.

"Let me help you, Maxxy," said Gran, lifting the top of the pillow. "Maybe we'll need to take some more stuffing out of there so that it isn't so heavy."

When Max was on his feet again and Maggie's shade was good as new, Maggie realized that the twins had arrived. "Ava! Are you feeling better?"

Ava nodded. "Finally," she said with a bright smile.

"And what did you do to your hair?" Maggie asked, walking around Ava in a circle.

"I straightened it!" said Ava proudly. "We did Bella's, too."

Bella put a hand to her head, suddenly self-conscious. But Maggie took one look and nodded her approval. "It looks really good," she said. "From the back, you two almost look like Gabby now!"

Ava glanced around the shop. "Where is Gabby?" she asked. "I can't wait to see her costume!"

Maggie frowned. "I think she's still working on that," she said.

"Really?" said Ava.

No, not really, thought Bella sadly. The truth was, Gabby hadn't had any time to think about a new costume. Bella had just told her last night, after dance class, that she'd be wearing the yellow Prommy dress. She couldn't even give Gabby the Betty Boot costume to wear because there was still too much work to do on it—sewing sequins and tying tassels.

So when Gabby came into the shop from the back room, she was wearing . . . jeans and a T-shirt. But she smiled all the same and *ooh*ed and *ahh*ed over all the other costumes.

"Won't that shade stay on your head?" she asked Maggie, who was still holding her lampshade.

"It did," said Maggie, "before Slick Breadstick ran me over and dented it." She glared at Max and then asked Gabby, "Did you and Papa find the last part of my costume?"

Gabby nodded. "I think so."

When Papa came out of the back room, he was blowing dust off a short black extension cord. "Will this work?" he asked. "I had to dig pretty far behind Gran's desk to get it."

Bella giggled, noticing the cobweb dangling off Papa's ginger-red mustache. When his face was red from working hard, like it was now, he looked like Papa Tomato, one of her favorite Shopkins characters. That's why Maggie had given him the name "Papa" in the first place.

"Thanks!" Maggie said, holding the cord up to measure its length. "Wait, do you have duct tape, too?"

Papa sighed, pulling out his hankie to wipe his face. "You're sure working your poor grandpa," he said, winking at her before disappearing into the back again.

"Hey, what're you doing with that cord?" asked Max, leaning against the train table. He looked hot in his costume, his cheeks almost as pink as Papa's.

"Every lamp needs a cord," said Maggie, as if he'd asked something silly. "Gotta plug me in, right?"

But when Papa helped Maggie tape the cord to her back, Max pointed and laughed. "You look like a lion," he said. "With a really long tail."

He's right, thought Bella. But she didn't want to say so.

Maggie whirled around to check out her tail. "Ugh," she said. "That's not going to work.

Lamps don't have tails. Papa, can we tape it somewhere else?"

Papa stroked his mustache and then adjusted the cord so that it was hanging off Maggie's side instead of her *back*side.

"Better?" she asked Max.

He nodded—which just about made him fall forward again. As the tall pillow teetered, Gabby reached out a quick hand to steady it.

"Now that you are all dressed," said Gabby, "I have a special announcement to make."

The room quieted down right away. *What is it?* wondered Bella. *Is Gabby going to say that she's not going to the party because she doesn't have a costume?* A wave of guilt rose in Bella's chest.

Gabby cleared her throat and said, "I've decided that instead of dressing up like a Shopkin tomorrow, I can be the announcer. You know, like in the Shopkins 'Beauty Pageant' cartoon, where Lippy Lips introduces all the pageant contestants?"

Bella smiled with relief. Gabby knew all the Shopkins cartoons by heart, and she was really good at acting them out. If she could do that tomorrow, she would still have fun—even if she didn't have a costume to wear.

Gabby raised her hand to her mouth as if she were holding a microphone. "Hello, and welcome to the Shopville Costume Contest finals," she said in a high Lippy Lips voice. "Slick Breadstick hails from the bakery aisle and is a favorite contestant this year." She waved her arm toward Max as if inviting him to walk the runway.

"Take a little walk, Max," said Maggie, nudging him.

He did. His skinny legs and black, dressy shoes looked funny under the giant pillow, but he managed to walk down the toy aisle and even spin around without falling down—or knocking anything over.

As the girls clapped and cheered, Max seemed pretty proud, especially when Ellie called out, "Nice mustache!"

"Bun Bun Slipper is our next contestant," said Gabby, waving at her little sister. "Take a hop down the bunny aisle, Miss Bun Bun."

Ellie didn't have to be told twice. She got down on all fours and sprang down the aisle, her bunny ears wiggling above her head.

"And where is our lovely Lana Lamp?" asked Gabby, glancing over her shoulder at Maggie.

"Oh," said Maggie, quickly putting the lampshade back on her head. "Here I am!"

As she started down the aisle, she swung her hips from side to side like a true fashion model. But the extension cord dangling from her side swung a bit *too* much. It got tangled up in her legs, making Maggie trip.

"Oops," she said, giggling as she righted herself.

"Lovely. Truly lovely," said Gabby, dabbing at her eyes as if she'd been moved to tears. "And you win extra points, Lana Lamp, for your superb grace and showmanship."

Maggie curtsied, pulling her gown out at the sides and bowing her head—which made the lampshade fall off.

Bella laughed along with everyone else, until she realized that she and Ava were next in line.

"Last, but not least," said Gabby, "we have two sisters looking perfectly pretty in their matching Prommy dresses."

Bella's palms started to sweat. Even though she was surrounded by friends, she didn't like everyone staring at her, especially when she was wearing such an uncomfortable outfit.

Ava, on the other hand, looked *perfectly* comfortable. She took a few steps ahead of Bella, did a graceful curtsy, and then walked down the aisle, waving to the others as if she were a princess in a parade.

How can she walk so fast in these things? Bella wondered, staring at the heels on her own shoes.

When she tried to take a step, her heel snagged the carpet. So she stood still.

"Bella!" Ava whispered, suddenly noticing that her sister wasn't beside her. She hurried back to the start of the aisle. "C'mon!" She linked arms with Bella and pulled her forward.

"Prommy has found her perfect match," said Gabby. "Aren't they elegant, ladies and gentleman? Such perfect poise and grace."

Right about then, Bella took a very *ungraceful* step . . . and felt her ankle wobble beneath her.

She reached out to grab something—anything!—for support. What she found was a stack of books on the rainbow bookshelf, which slid right off into her hands.

On the way down to the floor, Bella hit her forehead on the shelf, felt her foot slip out of her shoe, and heard a distinct *rrrip.*

Chapter Seven

Bella sat up, rubbing her right eye.

"Oh, no," she heard Ava groan.

"I'm okay," Bella said quickly, "At least, I think I am." She tried opening her eye but couldn't. It was watering too much.

"Your dress!" said Ava, squatting down and pointing. Yellow strings dangled from the torn hem.

Bella couldn't look. Her eye was starting to throb.

"Let me see, dear," said Gran, squatting beside her. "Clear out of the way, girls."

Gran tenderly pressed her fingers around Bella's eye, which she still couldn't open. "It's not bleeding," said Gran, "but I bet you'll have a bruised eye by morning. Maggie, can you get us a cold, wet paper towel, please?"

Maggie jumped up, but Ava stayed right by Bella's side. She stared into Bella's good eye and said sweetly, "Are you okay?"

Bella nodded, but she couldn't speak. She was afraid she was going to cry.

Gran sat beside them both and said soothingly, "You two sisters are quite a pair. We finally get Ava healthy again, and then Bella takes a terrific fall."

"That *was* quite a fall," said Gabby from behind them. She was using her regular voice now instead of her Lippy Lips voice.

"She fell just like Kooky Cookie did in the Shopkins cartoon!" said Ellie, who remembered the episodes almost as well as her big sister did. "Except Kooky Cookie did a somersault and got right back up again."

Bella laughed out loud, which felt better than crying. "A somersault? Why didn't I think of that?" she said, wiping her nose.

"I think your dress got in the way," said Max, sitting down cross-legged on the floor in front of her. Sitting looked a whole lot easier than standing in his Slick Breadstick costume.

Then Bella remembered the dress—and the horrible ripping sound she'd heard. She glanced down, and sure enough, the hem of her dress was torn. She could stick her fingers clear through the hole.

"So, I'm going to the prom with a torn dress and a black eye," Bella thought out loud. Her eyes burned again with hot tears.

"Mom can fix the dress," Ava reassured her.

"And this might help your black eye," said Maggie, returning with a cold paper towel for Bella to press against it.

Gran sighed. "We can't fix your eye overnight," she said. "But maybe we can cover it up." She stepped past the bookshelf to a spinning rack of wings, tutus, and other dress-up things. Beneath the sparkly tiaras were decorated masks on stretchy strings. "How about this one?" Gran asked, pulling a satiny yellow mask from the hook.

"Ooh . . ." Ava breathed from beside Bella. "Do you have a pink one, too?"

Gran squatted down to reach the lower hooks. "Sure do," she said, straightening back up. She held out a pink mask with sparkly sequins.

"We should both wear them!" said Ava.

"We should *all* wear them," said Gabby, leaning around Gran to reach for a white mask.

Pretty soon Gabby, Ava, and Bella were all trying on their masks in front of the mirror in the storage room. Putting on the mask hurt Bella's eye a little, but she was glad to know that everyone at the party wouldn't be staring at her bruise.

"How do we look?" asked Gabby. She turned around to model her mask for Maggie, who had just stepped into the room.

Maggie shook her head in disbelief. "With Ava's and Bella's hair straightened like that," she said, "you three could be triplets!"

Triplets? thought Bella. She couldn't even imagine it.

But Gabby said, "Cool! I always wanted twin sisters."

"Hey," said Ellie, bunny-hopping into the room. "You already have a sister!"

Gabby laughed and took off her mask. "You're right, Ellie. And one of you is more than enough." She reached down and wiggled one of Ellie's bunny ears.

Bella woke up Saturday morning with a feeling of dread in the pit of her stomach.

Ava was already up, probably because she was too excited about the costume party to sleep. *I wish I felt that way*, thought Bella. But her eye still hurt too much. And she wasn't any more excited about wearing her Prommy costume today than she'd been yesterday when she'd tripped in it and nearly ruined it.

As she stumbled into the kitchen, feeling as if she were sleepwalking, Mom and Ava both turned around from the counter.

"Oh, dear," said Mom, stepping quickly toward Bella. "Look at that eye!"

"It's green!" said Ava.

"And blue," said Mom.

"And purple," added Bella, staring into the side of the stainless steel toaster. The lid of her eye felt a little puffy, too.

"How about some more ice?" asked Mom.

Bella nodded and settled on the stool by the kitchen counter. As Mom scooped ice into a plastic bag, Bella stared at the bowl of fruit sitting in front of her. The banana was brown and bruised like her eye. But the apple beside it was shiny and red.

Apple, thought Bella, picturing the horse she'd befriended last weekend. It was Saturday morning, and Maggie was probably visiting Apple again. The thought perked Bella right up.

As soon as Ava went to take her shower, Bella asked her mom if she could go bike riding. She wasn't sure why she didn't wait to invite Ava to come—maybe because Ava wasn't all that into horses. Or maybe because it was nice to have something of her own, something that was all Bella's—and that didn't have to be shared.

Mom studied Bella's face. "The fresh air might do you good," she said. "But take your phone, and don't be gone too long."

Bella got dressed quickly, hoping Ava would still be showering by the time she left. She grabbed a sweatshirt from the hall closet, tucked her cell phone into her jeans, and hurried out the front door.

The fall air nipped at her nose, and her eye started watering again. But the thought of seeing Apple made her pedal faster, and before she knew it, she was turning onto the gravel road that led to the stable.

Bella saw Apple instantly. The horse was standing in the nearest corner of the pasture just inside the fence—as if he was waiting for her.

Wait, is that Starburst? she wondered, wanting to be sure this time. But as she set her bike down in the grass and stepped carefully toward the fence, the horse didn't run away.

And the patch of fur above his gentle eyes was shaped more like a triangle than a star.

"Hey, buddy," said Bella softly. "How are you?"

He nickered in response, which made her laugh. "Is that your way of saying hello?" she asked. "Or are you telling me to bring on the apples?"

She crossed the patch of grass between her and the nearest apple tree, and then bent down and filled her sweatshirt pockets with the reddest apples, making sure none of them were too bruised or wormy.

Apple pawed at the ground with his foot, as if to say, "Hurry up already!"

"I'm coming, I'm coming!" Bella joked, choosing the best apple and placing it on her outstretched palm.

Apple didn't waste any time taking it from her, but she noticed how gentle his mouth was on her hand. He was hungry, but he didn't want to accidentally bite her.

"Good boy," she said, giving him another.

After the third apple, Bella reached out to stroke the side of Apple's neck. He closed his eyes halfway like he was enjoying it. "You like that, don't you buddy?" she said.

He nickered back.

Bella laughed. "You sure talk a lot," she said. "But you're also really easy to talk to, you know that?"

He pricked his ears forward, as if to say, "I'm all ears."

So Bella talked. She told him about the costume contest. She told him that she had a sister who looked like her, just like Apple had a brother who looked like him. She told him how much Ava wanted to go to the contest dressed as Prommy. Then Bella told him how much she *didn't* want to do that.

When she paused, Apple sighed—actually sighed just like a human. Then his neck and head muscles shuddered, as if he couldn't stand the thought of his friend Bella going to the party in a prom dress.

"I know!" said Bella. "You get it, don't you, Apple?" she said, reaching out to stroke his neck again. "I wish I could just go as Betty Boot. I'd so much rather be a horseback rider."

She took a deep, shaky breath. Then she looked into Apple's gentle eyes and asked, "What should I do?"

The horse pawed at the ground in response. Then he trotted away from the fence, whinnied, and suddenly bucked his back feet into the air.

Bella's heart skipped a beat. She took a quick step backward—away from the fence.

"Apple!" someone called. It was Jessie, coming out of the stable with Maggie behind her, her red ponytail bobbing with each step.

Bella was relieved to see them. Had she just upset Apple somehow? If so, Jessie would know what to do.

"Wow," said Maggie as she and Jessie got closer. "Apple really wants to play."

"Is that what he's telling me?" asked Bella, watching the horse trotting around the pasture. Every now and then he would stop and look back at her.

"Yes," Jessie said, laughing. "I think he wants you to come out there and play *with* him." She crouched down to pick up an apple and dropped it into the burlap sack at her side.

Bella grinned. "I guess he answered me then."

Maggie cocked her head and asked, "What was your question?"

"I asked him what I should do about the costume party tonight," Bella confessed. "I think he's telling me that I should go as Betty Boot, if that's what I want to do."

"Well, of course you should," said Maggie, putting her hands on her hips. "I've been telling you that all along!" Then she took a step closer, staring at Bella's face. "You might need to wear a cowgirl mask, though," she added. "Look at that black eye!"

Bella sighed. "I know. It's not pretty. But I need more than a mask. I never did finish my cowgirl costume. I mean, the boots are all wrong. And the dress is really plain."

Jessie, who was still gathering apples from beneath the tree, stood up straight. "What kind of a costume are you putting together?"

"One like yours," Maggie explained. "Bella saw the picture of you when you were little in the stable, the one where you're in that white riding dress. She's trying to make one like it."

Jessie chuckled. "Why make your own? I still have that dress. I'd be happy to lend it to you—I mean, if it fits."

Bella felt a jolt of energy run from her head to her toes. "Really?" She tried not to shriek. "Do you think it would fit me?"

Jessie studied Bella's height. "I think it just might." She smiled. "I'll run into the house now and get it."

As Jessie headed back toward the stable and the white house beyond, Bella's mind raced. She could already picture herself in that beautiful costume. Then she pictured something else: Ava, standing at the party alone, a pink Prommy without her match.

"I just wish there was a way to do what I want to do without hurting Ava's feelings," Bella said. "She won't have fun at the party unless she's there with her twin."

Maggie nodded, biting into a ripe apple. "Too bad you can't clone yourself," she said, chewing slowly. "You need a triplet sister, one to do whatever Ava wants to do so that you can do your own thing."

As soon as the word *triplet* was out of Maggie's mouth, an idea started tickling the back of Bella's mind.

"What about Gabby? You said that Gabby, Bella, and I looked like triplets with our masks on."

"Totally," said Maggie, nodding. "With masks on and your hair straight like that—if Gabby were wearing the Prommy dress, people would think she was you!"

Bella bit her lip. *Some people might, but Ava would know in a second that it wasn't me.*

She stared out into the pasture, where Apple and Starburst were grazing side by side. From a distance, she couldn't see the white marks on their foreheads. She couldn't reach out her hand to tell which horse was friendlier. She couldn't tell them apart at all.

"Maybe it *could* work," Bella said, perking back up. "At least, for a little while. If Gabby and I keep our distance from Ava. And by the time Ava does find out, well, hopefully we'll all be having fun by then—and she won't care so much."

As the plan took shape in Bella's mind she wanted to paw at the ground—to buck up her legs like Apple, playing in the field. But first, she had to try on that cowgirl costume. *And* talk to Gabby.

Chapter Eight

"Bella, sit still, would you?" said Ava. "Mom can't get your hair straight if you aren't even *sitting* straight."

Bella sat up tall, hoping that if she did what Ava wanted, this whole hair straightening thing would be over soon. They were meeting Maggie at Teasley Toys in an hour to carpool to the party. Time was running out!

Mom set down the flatiron and used a brush to smooth Bella's hair away from her face. Then she covered Bella's eyes and spritzed her hair with hairspray. Bella wanted to cough from the smell, but she held it in.

"Ta-da!" said Mom. "All done."

"Wait!" said Ava. "She needs her head-band and her mask." Ava slid Bella's yellow headband into place and handed her the yellow mask. "Now try not to mess up your hair when you put the mask on. We don't have time for Mom to start all over again."

Bella slid the elastic cord over her head carefully, partly to protect her hairdo and partly to protect her black eye, which still hurt.

Then she turned to the mirror. The mask hid her bruised eye perfectly. *Phew!*

"Beautiful," said Mom. "Why don't you two use the mirror in my room so that you can see how you look side-by-side?"

Standing in front of Mom's bedroom mirror, the two girls studied their costumes. They wore sleeveless gowns with poufy skirts that swished just below their knees. Thin headbands held back their smooth, shiny hair. And the big bows sewn to the backs of their dresses looped out at their sides like giant wings.

We look like butterflies, thought Bella. *One pink, one yellow.* She didn't mind wearing the Prommy outfit right now—not when she knew she'd be swapping it out for the Betty Boot costume very soon.

"How do your shoes feel?" Ava asked.

Bella nodded. "Much better," she said, with a half-smile. After Bella had wiped out wearing heels at Teasley Toys, Ava had agreed to wear flats to the party.

Bella wiggled her toes inside her satiny shoes. They were comfortable, but they also made her feel guilty. Ava was being *so* nice, which made it harder for Bella to stick to her costume-swapping plan.

The ring of the telephone made both girls jump. They heard Mom talking in the kitchen. She popped her head into the doorway. "That was Maggie. She says remember to bring your Shopkins."

"Oh, yeah!" said Ava. "We need to show the contest judges what Shopkins are, so that they understand our costumes."

"Right," said Bella, licking her finger to smooth back a tiny stray curl at her temple. Her hair had to be absolutely straight; otherwise, it wouldn't look like Gabby's. And then the plan wouldn't work.

An hour later, when Mom pulled the minivan up in front of Teasley Toys, Bella noticed that the shop windows were dark. A CLOSED sign hung on the front door.

"Where are Gran and Papa?" she asked, following Ava out of the minivan.

A car door opened behind them, and Maggie popped out of the back seat, her lampshade in hand. "Weird, huh?" she asked, gesturing toward the dark toy shop windows. "Gran and Papa *always* stay open till seven o'clock on Saturdays. I wanted them to see our finished costumes. I finally got my cord just right."

Maggie spun to the side to show Ava and Bella her cord, which had been taped so that it hung much higher than before—and wouldn't get tangled in her legs.

"Maggie!" Max's voice whined from the car.

"Oh, sorry, Max," said Maggie, hurrying back. She helped her breadstick brother get his tall head out of the car and then steadied him once he reached the sidewalk.

"Jeepers," said Ava with a grin. "Good thing we have a minivan. C'mon, Max. I'll help you in."

While Ava got Max settled in the back of Mom's van, Bella turned to Maggie. "Is Gabby all ready?" she whispered.

Maggie nodded. "The Betty Boot costume fits her," she said. "We got this thing made in the shade." She set the lampshade on her head and squeezed something inside, which made light glow out of the top.

"Cool!" said Bella. "How'd you do that?"

"It's a flashlight," said Maggie, lifting the shade so that Bella could see the long, skinny light taped inside—with more duct tape. "I got the idea this afternoon. And it works!"

Bella nodded. "It definitely works."

Will our costume-swapping plan work, too? she wondered. *So far, so good.*

Music streamed out the front door of the community center. As Bella and her friends stepped through the doors and into the gym, a fairy flew by with a magic wand. Two pirates battled it out in front of the punch bowl with plastic swords. The lights were dim, and balloons bobbed above the snack table. The costume party was in full swing.

"Look for Gabby and Ellie!" said Maggie, taking the lead as they jostled their way through the crowd.

Bella searched the room for the golden-yellow cowboy hat. She'd know it anywhere—she'd been thinking about it ever since Jessie presented it to her at the stable that morning.

There were crowns and jester hats, wigs and witch hats, but no cowboy hats. Where was Gabby?

As Bella spun in a circle, she bumped smack into a giant red belly. *Uff!* She bounced back, trying not to fall.

"Papa Tomato!" said Ava, helping her sister find her balance.

Sure enough, that giant red belly belonged to someone in a Papa Tomato costume, and one look at the eyes behind those glasses told the sisters who it was: Maggie's grandpa!

Maggie spotted him right away, too. "Papa!" she said, laughing. "What are you doing here? And where'd you get that costume?"

Papa's red tomato costume was stuffed with squishy foam. Beneath his straw hat, he wore a leafy, green wig that looked like a tomato stem. The rest of the costume was all him, from his little round glasses to his red cheeks and mustache.

Papa winked at Maggie. "We heard they needed chaperones at this party, so Gran and I thought we'd get in on the fun."

That's when Bella noticed the woman at his side wearing a purple checkered bonnet and poster board shaped like a jar of grape jam. She wore one wide piece of board in front of her and one behind, so when she turned around to greet the girls, she bumped into two or three kids standing nearby.

"Excuse me. Pardon me," she said, her cheeks flushed. And then, "Surprise, girls!"

Maggie shook her head, grinning. "I can't believe you didn't tell us!" she said.

Gran's eyes twinkled behind her lavender glasses. "I think surprises are much more fun, don't you?"

Maggie nodded, laughing.

I hope Ava feels the same way about our surprise, thought Bella. Her sister was smiling, poking Papa's squishy, red belly with her finger. That seemed like a good sign.

When Bella saw the golden-yellow cowboy hat bobbing in her direction, she quickly forgot about Ava. Gabby was here!

Gabby dodged her way through the crowd with a cowgirl swagger, the spurs on her white boots jingling and her white skirt swishing from side to side. Luckily, Gabby had remembered to wear her white mask, too.

Does she look like me? wondered Bella. She just couldn't tell.

"Gabby!" said Ava as the cowgirl got closer. "You found a costume. You look really good!"

Bella felt a niggle of pride. *Ava likes my costume!* she thought. But then she had to remind herself that it wasn't *hers* yet. The hard part of the plan was still coming.

No one could see Ellie at first, until Gabby reached down and pulled her bunny rabbit sister up off the floor. "Don't hop down there," said Gabby. "Someone might step on you."

Ellie stood up, but she kept her arms bent at her chest like rabbit paws. She had painted her nose black, and somehow glued on little white whiskers.

Max wobbled over in his breadstick costume and patted Ellie on the head. "What a nice Bun Bun," he said.

Ellie wiggled her nose, which made Max laugh.

"Well," said Maggie, "I think we all look *brilliant.*" She reached inside the shade and turned on the flashlight again, which made the lamp glow bright in the dim party room.

"Ha!" said Ellie, admiring Lana Lamp. "I get it."

"Get what?" asked Max.

"Ellie got my joke," said Maggie. "You're really smart, Ellie. Or should I say, you're really *bright*?" She flickered the flashlight off and on again.

Ellie threw her bunny ears back and laughed.

"I'm smart, too!" said Max, his cheeks turning red.

"You are, Maxxy," said Gran, patting his breadstick back. "You are. And all of you do look positively brilliant. Let's hope the judges agree! The contest starts in half an hour."

Bella checked the clock nervously. She wanted to win the contest, for sure. But she was more excited about what would happen afterward: when she and Gabby would meet in the restroom to swap costumes. Then she could spend the rest of the night as Betty Boot.

Bella glanced at Gabby, who was grinning at her from beneath that golden-yellow cowboy hat. Gabby's eyes were twinkling. She looked excited, too.

"Wait," said Maggie, holding up her hands. "Did everyone bring their Shopkins? We have to remember to show the judges how our costumes match our Shopkins characters."

Bella slipped her hand into the pocket Mom had sewn into the Prommy dress. "I've got mine," she said, holding it up.

But in the light shining from Maggie's lampshade head, Ava noticed something—something important.

"Hey, that's not your yellow Prommy," she said loudly. "That's Betty Boot!"

Bella glanced down and sucked in her breath. Sure enough, she was holding a little white cowboy boot—a boot that most certainly did not match her yellow Prommy dress.

Chapter Nine

"Oops!" said Bella, dropping Betty Boot back into her pocket as if she were a hot little potato. "That's not Prommy."

"I'll say," said Ava. "Wow, Bella. You're such a space case sometimes."

Bella shrugged, feeling as if she were sinking into a pile of quicksand. Luckily, Maggie and Gabby were there to pull her back out.

"Did you bring that Shopkin for me?" Gabby asked Bella brightly. "I don't have Betty Boot in my collection."

Ava's eyes widened. "Oh!" she said. "Is that who you are, Gabby? Are you Betty Boot? How perfect!"

Perfect is right, thought Bella, reaching back into her pocket for Betty Boot. She shot Gabby a grateful smile.

"Anyway, I knew you didn't have Prommy in your pocket, Bella," said Ava. "Because I grabbed her for you." She reached into her own pocket and pulled out two tiny high-heeled shoes—one pink and one yellow. She handed the yellow one to Bella.

Phew! thought Bella. *Sometimes having a super-organized sister is a good thing.*

When it was time for costume judging, all the kids in the gym lined up like one long parade. Superheros and princesses marched past the judges: three adults sitting at a low table.

As the Shopkins Kids Club took their turn, Gran and Papa helped. They brought the Shopkins to the judges, one by one, as each kid walked by. "This is Pink Prommy," Bella heard Gran announce, handing a shoe to the judges. "And this is her match: Yellow Prommy."

Bella's knees wobbled beneath her as she followed Ava past the judges' table. *Thank goodness I'm not wearing high heels,* she thought, feeling steadier in her satin flats.

And before Bella knew it, the contest was over. The last little kid, dressed in a peapod costume, walked past the judges' table. And then the judges led everyone in applause for what they called "big creativity in costume making."

"Did we win?" asked Max, his face not just red, but sweaty now.

"We don't know yet, Max," said Maggie. "We have to be patient and wait. It could take a while." Max crossed his arms and sat down on the gym floor. Patience wasn't exactly one of his super strengths.

It's not mine, either, thought Bella. She glanced at Gabby. *Should we go now?* she tried to say with her eyes, nodding toward the restrooms.

Gabby nodded, tipping her cowboy hat low over her eyes.

It was time.

The Betty Boot costume felt so different from the Prommy dress—heavier and more *real,* somehow. Bella liked the boots best, the way the heels clicked against the tile floor of the restroom. She checked the mirror three times before she finally poked her head out the door to make sure the coast was clear.

Gabby had already gone back to the party, looking like a princess in the yellow Prommy dress. So now it was Bella's turn.

She was thrilled to see that the lights in the gym were back down low now that the costume contest was over. *If I stay away from Ava,* thought Bella, *this just might work.*

She found Maggie standing by the snack table, trying to drink a cup of punch without the shade falling off her head. "Hey, Gabby!" she said, catching sight of the Betty Boot costume.

Bella giggled. "It's me," she whispered.

Maggie choked on her drink, dribbling punch down her front. "Oops," she said, wiping her chin. "Is that really you in there, Bella?"

Bella nodded. "Sorry I surprised you," she said, reaching for a napkin. "Good thing the punch is the same color as your dress."

"Who cares about that?" asked Maggie, setting down the cup. "Look at you! I really, truly, *totally* thought you were Gabby. Honest!" She grabbed Bella's hands and bounced up and down, her lamp cord swinging from side to side.

"Good!" said Bella. "That's what I was hoping for. Where's Ava?"

Maggie scanned the crowd and then pointed. "She's dancing with Ellie in the corner."

When Bella saw the pink Prommy dancing next to Bun Bun Slipper, she released her breath. Ava was having fun and *not* missing her sister—at least not yet.

Bella reached for a cup of punch, but then looked down at her white dress and changed her mind. "Should we dance, too?" she asked Maggie, feeling like Apple in the pasture, ready to play.

"Yes!" said Maggie. "Follow me." She turned on the light in her lampshade and boogied toward the dance floor, swinging her cord in her hand. Bella was glad that Maggie went to the other corner of the gym, away from Ava.

Dancing in a Betty Boot costume was almost as much fun as Bella imagined it would be. She shimmied her shoulders beneath her cowboy hat. She swayed her hips, her white dress swinging from side to side. She stepped in her shiny leather boots, hearing the *jingle* of her spurs.

But when she saw a pink Prommy dress heading her way, she ducked down low. "Ava's coming!" she said.

Maggie stood on tiptoe, lifting her shade to see better. "Uh-oh," she said. "I think she's looking for you. Just keep dancing."

Bella spun in a half-circle, turning her back to Ava.

"Hey, Maggie. Hey, Gabby," she heard Ava say. "Have you seen Bella?"

Don't look at her, Bella told herself. *Don't look at her!* Instead, she kept her back turned and shook her head no.

"I think she might be, um, over by the balloons," said Maggie. "By Max, over there somewhere."

"Okay, thanks!" Ava said brightly.

When the coast was clear, Bella turned around again. But now she didn't feel so much like dancing. "I think I'll sit down for a while," she told Maggie.

Maggie shrugged. "Okay," she said. "But, Bella? You look great."

Bella smiled—wide. The costume did look great. So why didn't she *feel* great inside? Was it because they had just lied to Ava?

The music stopped suddenly, and the speakers in the gym crackled. "Princesses and pirates," a man with a deep voice said, "the judges have made their decisions! We will now announce the winners of the individual and group costume contests. If you hear your name, please approach the judges' table."

Maggie grabbed Bella's arm. "This is it!" she said, squeezing tight.

The individual costume winners came first, with third prize going to one of the pirates. Second prize went to a witch with a green face and a long crooked nose. And first prize went to . . . Slick Breadstick!

"That's Max!" said Maggie. "Maxxy!" She pushed through the crowd toward the judges' table. Bella followed close behind, keeping her eyes peeled for a pink Prommy dress.

Gran Jam helped Max toward the table, holding his tall breadstick head steady. Maggie ran up from behind and hugged him, almost knocking him off balance. When he came away from the table, he was proudly holding what looked like a pumpkin trophy.

Bella barely heard the next announcement: third-place winners for group costumes. But she heard the second-place winners loud and clear: the Shopkins Kids Club!

Bella's heart raced as she watched her friends, one by one, approach the table. There was Ava, her head spinning wildly from side to side.

She's looking for me, thought Bella sadly. *What do I do now?*

Someone nudged her from behind: Gabby, in her yellow Prommy dress. "We have to go, too," she whispered. "We'll stick together and make it quick."

Gabby held Bella's hand as they hurried toward the table. Bella tried not to look directly at Ava, but she caught the smile on her face when she spotted the yellow Prommy dress coming her way. As Ava walked toward them, Gabby pulled Bella's hand hard to the left, and they ducked to the other side of Maggie, Ellie, and Max.

Maggie accepted the award for the group: a big pumpkin trophy with the words FALL FESTIVAL COSTUME WINNERS engraved across the bottom. She held it up high while the other kids in the gym clapped. And as she led her friends away from the table, she took a little bow—which sent the lampshade tumbling to the floor, just as Bella took a step in her riding boots.

Crunch.

"Oh, no!" said Bella, bending quickly to pick up the shade. It was dented in the shape of a cowboy boot. And the frame inside was broken.

Maggie just shrugged. "We already won," she said. "It doesn't matter." When she put the shade back on her head, it slid all the way down to rest on her shoulders.

"Ha!" said Max, pointing. "You look funny."

Maggie put her hands on her hips, pretending to be mad. "I think I look like a *queen*," she said. "Don't they wear collars like this?"

Max shook his breadstick head. "Nope," he said. "You look like a dog with a cone on its head."

That did it—Bella burst out laughing. And when she did that, Ellie whirled around to face her.

"Hey," she said, scrunching up her bunny nose. "You're not Gabby. You're Bella."

Uh-oh. Bella's ears buzzed as if a fluorescent lamp had just turned on overhead. Not all of the eyes in the room were on her—most of the kids had gone back to eating and dancing. But one pair of eyes was definitely zoomed in on Bella: Ava's confused, wide-set eyes.

Ava lifted the pink mask from her face and stared.

"Bella?" she asked in a small voice. "Is that you?"

Chapter Ten

It all fell apart, Bella thought, sitting in the hallway with her back against the wall. She and her friends were waiting just outside the restroom, music still pounding from the gym next door. Ava was inside the restroom—and wouldn't come out.

Maggie held her broken lampshade in her lap. And Max had taken off his breadstick costume entirely because it was way too hot. He still wore the beret on his head, along with his crooked mustache. And his cheeks were sweaty and bright red.

"You know," said Maggie, messing up his ginger-red hair. "You kind of look like Papa Tomato. Maybe next year you can go to the party as a tomato, too—a little cherry tomato."

Max stuck out his lower lip and blew his bangs off his forehead. "I want to be a tomato," he said, nodding. "Not a dumb breadstick."

"Hey, now," said Gran Jam, overhearing. "Slick Breadstick won first prize tonight, remember?"

Max perked back up and jumped to his feet. "Where's my trophy?" he asked.

"Papa is putting it in the car along with your breadstick costume," said Gran. "Don't worry, he'll take good care of it."

Just then, Ellie hopped down the hall, one ear dangling down over her face. "My ear broke," she said, taking off her headband. "Can you fix it, Gabby?"

Gabby, still in the yellow Prommy dress, reached for the headband and inspected the ear. "I think the wire broke," she told Ellie. "I'm sorry."

"Look on the bright side, Ellie," said Maggie. "I think your ears look kind of cute that way." She cocked her head, waiting for Ellie to smile. "Get it?" Maggie tried again. "Look on the *bright* side?" She pointed at her broken lampshade.

Ellie rolled her eyes. "No more dumb lamp jokes!" she huffed. Then she reached for her headband and tried again to make the broken ear stand up. When it wouldn't, her bottom lip quivered.

I know just how she feels, thought Bella.

Yes, everything had fallen apart. And the worst part was the look on Ava's face when she'd realized that Bella had tricked her.

Will she ever talk to me again? wondered Bella, taking off her cowboy hat and leaning back against the wall. Her head was starting to hurt.

Maggie stood up and pressed her ear to the restroom door. "Should I go in again?" she asked, glancing over her shoulder at Gran Jam.

Gran shook her head and said gently, "Let me try this time." She pressed open the door and turned sideways, trying to get her cardboard jam-jar body through the narrow entrance.

As the door closed behind her, Bella crossed her fingers. *Please let Ava come out,* she hoped. *Please don't let her be* too *mad at me.*

A few minutes later, Ava *did* come out, with Gran Jam behind her. Ava's mask dangled from the string around her neck, so Bella could see her tear-stained cheeks. Ava looked at her for just a moment before turning her face away and hurrying down the hall.

"Ava!" Bella said, standing up as quickly as she could. She opened her mouth to call after her sister, but the words stuck in her throat—which suddenly felt raw and kind of scratchy.

"It's okay," said Gran, putting a gentle hand on Bella's shoulder. "Let her go for now."

But Bella knew it wasn't okay. Ava was mad, really mad. And there was something else:

Bella was getting sick.

Serves me right, she thought sadly, swallowing the lump in her throat.

Sunday morning, Bella woke up with an aching head. And Ava was gone.

Ava stayed gone all day. While Mom took Bella to the doctor to get antibiotics, Ava went to visit Gran and Papa. When Bella went back to bed in the late afternoon, Ava was still gone. And when Bella woke up Monday morning, finally feeling well enough to sit up and suck on a Popsicle, Ava was already at school.

Suddenly, Bella knew just how Ava had felt when she was the one sick in bed: *lonely.* But Bella felt something else, too: guilt for lying to Ava and hurting her feelings.

So when Ava came into their bedroom Monday afternoon, carrying a bowl of ice cream, Bella sat up to greet her. Ava's hair framed her face in springy curls. She looked nothing like the smooth-haired pink Prommy from the costume party the other night.

"Mom said I had to bring this to you," said Ava in a flat voice. "Here." She set the ice cream on the bedside table and turned to leave.

"Ava," said Bella, her voice scratchy. "Wait. I'm really sorry."

Ava paused in the doorway. Was she going to walk away? Or would she stay and listen? Her shoulders heaved, like Apple's had when he let out that big sigh. Finally, Ava turned around.

"Why didn't you just tell me?" she asked, spreading her arms palms up. "Why couldn't you just say that you wanted to wear a different costume? Why did you have to lie to me and sneak around like that?"

Tears welled up in Bella eyes. *Because it was too hard! It was too hard to tell you.*

But sneaking around was hard, too. And seeing Ava so upset was the hardest part of all. When Bella opened her mouth, all she could say was, "I don't know."

Ava shook her head sadly. Then she turned and left the room, closing the door behind her.

By Tuesday, Bella was back at school, but Mom made her stay home from dance class. Ava was talking to Bella again, finally, but something had changed between them. Bella could feel it, like the way she could feel winter coming just by the chill in the air.

By Wednesday afternoon, Bella knew she had to do something. Maybe she couldn't tell Ava why she did what she did. But could she *show* her?

As they walked home from school in silence, Bella got an idea. "Ava," she asked, "will you ride bikes with me tonight? I want to show you something."

Ava shrugged. "Where are we going?"

Bella hesitated. "It's a surprise."

Ava stopped walking and looked at her. "Really? Another surprise? Maybe you should just tell me the truth this time."

It felt like a slap in the face, but Bella knew Ava was right. She took a deep breath. "I want to take you to meet a horse," she said, knowing that Ava might shoot that idea right down.

"His name is Apple. And he's why I wanted to go to the party as Betty Boot."

Ava stared at Bella for what felt like a long time, her hands on her hips. But finally her face softened, and she said, "Okay."

Mom gave them permission to go see Apple as long as they were back before the sun set. So the two girls set off on their bikes with Bella in the lead.

It felt funny for Bella to hear her sister's bike tires behind her for once. But it felt good, too—having something special to share with Ava. *I hope she likes Apple as much as I do,* thought Bella, pumping her pedals as fast as she could.

Apple wasn't waiting at the fence this time. Bella rode onto the grass and parked her bike against one of the apple trees. Ava rode in behind her, setting her bike down on the grass. "Where is he?" she asked, shivering and zipping up her jacket.

"He's around here somewhere," said Bella. "There, look!" She pointed out into the pasture, where both horses were grazing.

"There's two of them!" said Ava, stepping toward the fence.

"They're brothers," said Bella, smiling. "Almost twins."

At the word *twins,* Ava turned toward Bella. "I didn't know horses could be twins," she said.

Bella shrugged. "They look a lot alike," she said. "But they have really different personalities." *Like you and me*. But she thought saying so might hurt Ava's feelings.

When Bella turned to pick a ripe apple from the tree, she heard the sound of hooves trotting across the field behind her. Sure enough, Apple was there waiting when she turned around. Starburst was walking across the field, too, his ears pricked forward.

As Apple approached the fence, Ava took a step back.

"It's okay," said Bella. "He won't bite. He just wants an apple. See?" She showed Ava how to hold the apple on her palm. "You want to try?"

Ava shook her head, but she stepped toward the fence again. "How come the other horse won't come to you?" she asked.

"He's more scared of people," said Bella. "His name's Starburst."

Ava leaned against the fence and shaded her eyes to get a better look at Starburst. "That's kind of funny," she said. "He's afraid of people, and I'm . . . I'm kind of afraid of horses!"

Bella's jaw dropped open. Ava had never said that before—that she was *afraid* of horses. "I thought you just didn't like them!"

Ava shook her head. She turned away and started studying the apple tree, as if she was searching for the perfect apple. She chose one, plucked it from the branch, and rubbed it clean on the leg of her jeans.

Then Ava took a deep breath and said, "I get why you like horses so much, Bella. You should take lessons. I think you'd be a really good rider."

Bella raised her eyebrows. "Really?" she said. "But . . . what about dance?"

Ava shrugged. "You shouldn't do it if you want to do something else. It's okay for us to like different things."

It sounds so simple when she says it like that, thought Bella. She suddenly wanted to hug her sister. She was about to, when Ava held out the apple. "Will you show me how again?" she asked.

Bella grinned. "Sure. Just hold your hand out flat like this."

Ava looked scared—really scared—as Apple began eating the apple out of her hand. But then she giggled nervously. "It tickles!"

"I know," said Bella, laughing. "I like that part."

That was when she noticed that Starburst was coming closer. Would she be able to feed him out of her hand someday soon? Was he getting more brave?

Maybe we all are, thought Bella, watching her sister pick another apple from the tree.

Chapter Eleven

Bella chose her two-pack Shopkins basket from the display and hurried to the counter. "You're buying your own?" asked Gran, looking surprised. She wasn't wearing her Gran Jam costume anymore, but Bella could still picture her with that checkered purple bonnet.

"Yes!" Bella announced, digging in her pocket for her cash. "Ava and I are splitting up our Shopkins collection today. I'll have my own from now on."

Gran raised an eyebrow. "And that's . . . a good thing, right?"

Bella nodded. "Ava's not mad anymore," she whispered to Gran. "We made up."

Gran smiled wide. "Oh, good," she said. "That's the news I was hoping to hear." She popped open the cash register drawer and counted out Bella's change.

Then Bella hurried into the back room, where a few other members of the Shopkins Kids Club were waiting.

Ella wasn't wearing her bunny ears anymore, and she'd finally managed to wash the black face paint off her nose—although it had taken a few days. Bella's black-and-blue eye had almost gone back to its normal color, too. But as she looked around the storage room, there were plenty of reminders of the costume party.

Maggie's extension cord "tail" rested on Gran's desk, the duct tape still attached to one end. Papa's tomato outfit was tucked in the corner of the room, plump and fluffy like a beanbag chair. And the lamp in the room seemed particularly bright, since it had no shade.

"Here, Bella, you take Apple Blossom," said Ava, holding up the Shopkin from her place beside Gabby on the rug. "She's perfect for you!"

Bella laughed and took the little, green apple out of her sister's hand.

"Take Sugar Lump, too," said Ava, sorting through the Shopkins in her metal lunch box. "Horses love sugar cubes."

"They sure do," said Ellie, sitting cross-legged with her chin in her hands.

Ava poked through the pile again and said, "I'm guessing you don't want this one, though, right?" She lifted out a little shoe with a high heel and a pointed toe. It was Prommy—the yellow one.

Bella felt a pang of sadness, remembering the costume party. She swallowed hard.

"Actually," she said, reaching for the shoe, "I *do* want that one. Is that okay?"

Ava smiled. "Of course," she said. "That one will always feel like yours anyway. And now"—she dug through the pile and pulled out the matching pink shoe—"we'll still have Twinsies." She lifted both the pink Prommy and the yellow Prommy side by side and then placed the yellow one carefully in her sister's hand.

As Bella sat down beside her sister, she sorted through the lunch box and chose a few more Shopkins: Sweeps, because the broom reminded her of the one that Jessie used in Apple's stable; Rub-a-Glove, because that seemed like something horse groomers would use, too; and Carrie Carrot Cake.

"Let me guess," said Ava, raising a finger. "You took Carrie Carrot Cake because horses like carrots."

Bella nodded and burst out laughing.

That's when Maggie walked through the door. She did a double take when she saw the sisters. "Wow," she said. "I could have sworn that was Ava laughing in here. Bella, you sound just like your sister!"

"Really?" said Bella, catching her breath. "No one has ever said that before."

Ava threw her arm around Bella's shoulders. "See? We'll always share *some* things," she said.

"Like your curly hair?" asked Ellie.

Ava smoothed her hand over her curls. "I don't know," she said thoughtfully. "I was thinking about wearing mine straight again. How about it, Bella?"

Bella snorted. "Um, no thanks," she said quickly.

She worried at first that she'd hurt Ava's feelings, but Ava just laughed.

Then Max flew into the room like a tiny tornado. He was wearing a long-sleeved striped tee and his cargo pants—along with a crooked mustache.

"Hey, Slick," said Maggie, giggling. "It's about time you got here. Ready to open your Shopkins? You go first this week."

As Max tore open his two-pack, Bella propped up the plastic bag of Shopkins on her lap. Now that she had her own collection, she would need something to put it in. A Shopkins lunch box like her sister's maybe? *Or a horse lunch box,* she thought happily. *Then mine will look different.* She imagined the perfect picture on the front, a reddish brown horse eating an apple.

"Ava and Bella, it's your turn," said Maggie, breaking Bella's thoughts.

"Wait," said Ava. "Should we take two separate turns, now that we have our own collections?"

Bella shrugged. Something about that didn't feel quite right. "How about if we still open ours at the same time?"

Ava nodded happily. "Yes!"

They waited until they each held a crinkly yellow pouch in their hands. Then, on the count of three, the girls tore the pouches open.

A tiny cake dropped onto the floor in front of Bella—a chocolate cake with a strawberry and a dollop of cream on top. "Choco Lava!" she declared. "I don't have that one yet." She glanced over to see what Ava had opened.

"I think . . ." said Ava, lifting her own Shopkin, "that I got a cake, too." Hers was yellow. She studied the Shopkins checklist and said, "Wait, I got the other Choco Lava!"

She held hers out next to Bella's. The two cakes had the same berry and whipped cream on top. But Ava's had berry filling oozing out, and Bella's had chocolate filling.

"Hmm . . ." said Bella. "They look the same on the outside, but they're way different on the inside."

Ava knew just what she was saying. "Like us?" she asked, meeting Bella's eyes.

"Like us," said Bella. Then she tapped her Shopkin against Ava's. "Twinsies?"

"Twinsies," said Ava, smiling. She put her Choco Lava into her lunch box.

And Bella placed her Shopkin tenderly into her very own bag.